The Adventure of the Giant Bean

by G. H. Teed

First published in the Union Jack magazine,
No. 1031, 14 July 1923.

Illustrated by Val Reading

Stillwoods Edition

Stillwoods.Blogspot.Ca

Catalogue Information:
Title: The Adventure of the Giant Bean
Author: G. H. Teed
First published in the Union Jack magazine, No. 1031, 14 July 1923.
Illustrated by: Val Reading
This Edition by: Stillwoods, 2021
ISBN Canada: 978-1-989788-40-0
Blog: Stillwoods.Blogspot.Ca
Author Blog: http://ghteed.blogspot.com/
Storefront: http://www.lulu.com/spotlight/lulubook22

https://tinyurl.com/ve25d42s This link should go to a spreadsheet of all known Teed stories. The list is annotated with various information on the stories and my progress with recapturing the work. The library of Teed's stories increases almost weekly. Check at the **Lulu.Com** for the latest arrivals. Search for Teed./drf

Keywords: Sexton Blake, British fictional detective, Tinker, Wu Ling

Cautionary Note: This series of books by Stillwoods are intended to make the stories of G. H. Teed, born in New Brunswick, Canada, available to collectors and researchers. The editor, or rather digitizer has not altered the original publication.

This story may contain language and racial terms that are not appropriate to today. I apologize for them; I know that the author was using his voice to excite and entertain an adventurous English audience. These works were published from 82 to 110 years ago. Most every work has characters of redeeming ethnicity within.

I hope you enjoy and share these stories; I have.
Doug Frizzle

A story in the brilliant Yellow Beetle series —a yarn of peril and adventure in the Orient and in London. Those who have read previous tales of Prince Wu Ling and his Brotherhood versus Sexton Blake and Sir Gordon Saddler will welcome this as the latest in a really enthralling series.

NOTE. This story concerns the further incidents in the history of the Ling-tse Vase. For the benefit of those who are not already acquainted with the wonderful events that precede those here related, it is pointed out that previous stories concerning the Vase appeared in the "Union Jack" dated May 19th and June 9th last, under the titles of "The Tabu of Confucius" and "The Slave of the Thieves' Market" respectively. All three episodes, including the present one, are complete in themselves. — Editor.

Wu Ling and

G. H. TEED'S work in "THE UNION JACK"

No.

507   **The Brotherhood of the Yellow Beetle**   Prince Wu Ling.

510   **The Idol's Spell**   Wu Ling.

512   **The Yellow Sphinx**   Yvonne Cartier, Dr. Huxton Rymer, Wu Ling.

519   The White Mandarin. Wu Ling.

526   The Yellow Octopus. Dr. Huxton Rymer, Wu Ling.

529   **The Sacred Sphere**   Yvonne Cartier, Dr. Huxton Rymer, Wu Ling.

552   Pirated Cargo. Wu Ling.

564   The Crimson Pearl.   Yvonne Cartier, Dr. Huxton Rymer, San and The Brotherhood of the Yellow Beetle.

579   A Voice from the Dead.   San and the Brotherhood of the Yellow Beetle

596   The Case of the Poisoned Telephone. Wu Ling.

607   The Guest of the Grey Panther.   Wu Ling.

1000   **The Thousandth Chance**   The   Convention   at Abbey Towers of almost all Blake's adversaries and the first of a Wu Ling series.

1023   The Tabu of Confucius.   Prince Wu Ling.

1026   The Slave of the Thieves' Market.   Prince Wu Ling.

1031   **The Adventure of the Giant Bean**   Prince Wu Ling.

1064   The Street of Many Lanterns. Yvonne Cartier, Prince Wu Ling.

1086   The Case of the Strange Sickness.   Prince Wu Ling.

1224   The Adventure of the Yellow Beetle. Prince Wu Ling.

1225   **The Temple of Many Visions**   Prince Wu Ling.

1226   Doomed to the Dragon.   Prince Wu Ling.

1227   The House of the Wooden Lanterns. Prince Wu Ling.

1438   Yellow Guile. Dr. Huxton Rymer, Mary Trent and Prince Wu Ling.

1494   **Sexton Blake in Manchuria** Roxane   Harfield   & Prince Wu Ling.

1495   Arms to Wu Ling.

1497   The Blood Brothers of Nan-Ha.   Roxane Harfield & Prince Wu Ling.

"SEXTON BLAKE LIBRARY"

(First Series)

1 **The Yellow Tiger**   Yvonne Cartier, Prince Wu Ling and Baron Beauremon.

307   The Crimson Belt.   Dr. Huxton Rymer & Prince Wu Ling.

"SEXTON BLAKE LIBRARY"

(Second Series)

35 **The Case of the Mummified Hand** Yvonne   Cartier,   Dr. Huxton Rymer, Mary Trent, George Marsden Plummer, Prince Wu Ling, Prince Menes, The Three Musketeers & The Black Eagle.

277   The Yellow Skull.   George Marsden Plummer, Vali Mata-Vali & Prince Wu Ling.

BOLD indicates Stillwoods Edition available.   /drf

The Adventure of the Giant Bean

A story in the brilliant YELLOW BEETLE series—a yarn of peril and adventure in the Orient and in London. Those who have read previous tales of Prince WU LING and his Brotherhood versus SEXTON BLAKE and Sir GORDON SADDLER will welcome this as the latest in a really enthralling series.

It was a hot, murky night in the native town of Canton, and a heavy mist was hanging low on the river when two individuals, garbed in the habiliments of the Chinese aristocracy, emerged arm in arm from the Temple of Eternal Light, which stands near the Gate of the Tiger, and turned to the left, which would take them past the noisome and notorious Thieves' Market.

One was a gentleman of considerable age, as was evident from the stooping manner in which he walked; the other was considerably more youthful, as one could have guessed from his upright carriage and his firm, vigorous stride, even though it had been modified to suit the pace of his companion.

At the moment of emergence they were not speaking, but the elder of the pair was acting rather strangely for one who had just left the august portals of the greatest Buddhist temple in South China. He was laughing; and what made his mirth appear almost sinister was the fact that it was quite noiseless. It was an internal upheaval which left him shaking and fluttering as he supported himself on the arm of his companion.

They proceeded for some little distance in this fashion, during which the younger man kept darting his eyes to right and left as if seeking for signs of danger. The elder finally became aware of this, for he checked his unholy mirth long enough to say:

"They won't attack now, Blake. They had their drubbing in the slave hall of the Thieves' Market to-night, and, until morning at least, my men will be in control of the whole quarter. We shall not be molested before we reach the House of the Lord High August One of Two Hundred Intelligences."

"I hope you are right, Sir Gordon," responded Sexton Blake, for it was he. "I am not keen on getting mixed up in any further trouble to-night. I am anxious to return and find out how Tinker is progressing, after the torture he received at the hands of the sacrificial priest of the temple. And, besides, now that we have jockeyed the Ling-tse vase out of the possession of the Chuen-to-yan and Wu Ling, the sooner we get away from Canton the better."

As may have been gathered from the foregoing, Sexton Blake was discussing certain events which had taken place that day and evening in Canton. His companion was Sir Gordon Saddler, that strange old man of nearly ninety, who had been steeped in the mystery and intrigue of China for more than half a century, and who, for the past twenty years, had been living in the heart of the Chinese quarter of San Francisco, at the House of the Silver Moon, where he was known as the ever-to-be-respected Hsui-fsi —a wise patriarch, whose pure British blood was never for a moment, suspected.

Since Sexton Blake had started out on his memorable chase after the Ling-tse Vase, he and Sir Gordon had been working more or less in alliance.

This ancient vase, although it was no larger than a woman's thimble, was yet large enough to bear inside and outside a multitude of mysterious cabalistic signs, which made it of the deepest reverence to all Chinese, and which was, too, the most potent symbol of both temporal and spiritual power in China. In San Francisco, owing to the regrettable habit of taking opium which the "Mystery Man of 'Frisco" had contracted during his years in the East, and when the vase had been in his possession, his enemy, Wu Ling, had succeeded in getting possession of it, despite the fact that it was protected by the tabu of Confucius.

Sexton Blake had rushed across from London, and from 'Frisco the chase had led into Mexico and the Gulf of California, where, at the very moment when Wu Ling had been about to fall into his hands, Fate had snatched away Blake's victory.

On that occasion Blake, as well as Wu Ling, had thought the vase gone for good, although Blake did not know that as the explosion which had rent asunder the ship on which Wu Ling was escaping had hurled the prince into the water, it had at the same time torn from his grasp the precious Ling-tse vase. The last Wu Ling had seen of it was a brief sight of something sinking into the depths, and for some time after he firmly believed that it lay at the bottom of the Gulf of California. And what chance was there of ever finding such a tiny object among those deeps?

But he was mistaken, as was proved only a week or so after, for during a fishing expedition in the gulf, when Blake had hooked and landed a giant silver king tarpon, Blake made a startling discovery. This was nothing less than the sight of a small object in the stomach of the tarpon as Chan, the Chinese "boy" of Colonel Fairfax, with whom he was staying, cut the fish open. But Chan had seen and also recognised the vase, and by lightning sleight-of-hand work managed to secrete it about his person.

Before Blake could confide his suspicions to his host and ask him to act, Chan had made off and got clean away. But instead of being in Wu Ling's service Chan, it was discovered later, was in the service of the Chuen-to-yan, of the great Temple of Eternal Light, in Canton, whither Blake, Tinker, and Sir Gordon Saddler hastened.

The Chuen-to-yan was just as powerful in a religious way as Wu Ling was in a temporal way in China, for the Chuen-to-yan was supreme head of the Buddhists, a position equivalent there to the Pope among the Roman Catholics.

Thus it will be seen, a new and powerful factor had arisen with which Blake had to contend, and it was of the utmost urgency to regain possession of the Ling-tse vase if the peace of the East were to be maintained. With that in the possession of either Wu Ling or the Chuen-to-yan, no man could visualise the horror which would sweep over China, dragging millions into misery, rapine, and death.

Sexton Blake was too well conversant with China not to realise that single-handed he had little hope of discovering the whereabouts of the vase, or, even if he did, to recover it, once it had fallen into the hands of Wu Ling or the Chuen-to-yan.

Therefore he had more than welcomed the alliance with Hsui-fsi. for if there was one other person in China who controlled a force equal to that of either Wu Ling or the Chuen-to-yan, that person was Sir Gordon.

And although Hsui-fsi was much stronger in the north than in the south, he had proved during the past few days that his strength there, combined with the extraordinary Celestial twist of cunning which he had acquired during his long residence in China, when he had been mixed up in every one of the sinister intrigues of the old Court, was equal to the test to which it had been put.

When Tinker had been captured, and, after being given the lash by the chief sacrificial priest of the temple, had been taken to the underground slave-hall of the notorious Thieves' Market, to be sold as a slave for the rice-fields in the interior, Sir Gordon had summoned every man he controlled in Canton. They had attacked the Thieves' Market, had made a surprise stroke, and in the midst of the sanguinary melee which had followed had succeeded in rescuing Tinker.

Following that, they had bearded the Chuen-to-yan and Wu Ling in the former's secret apartments in the Temple of Eternal Light, and, by sheer daring, had managed to befool the wily pair of arch conspirators. As far as they knew now, the homing pigeon which Sir Gordon had smuggled into the temple, must have arrived at the House of Two Hundred Intelligences, and it was the thought of how he had outwitted the other pair that had filled the old man with such unholy glee.

But Blake was remembering how the vase had been lost in 'Frisco. He was recalling that Wu Ling had managed on that occasion to break the tabu, even though he himself had not sacrificed his own soul as the unfortunate victim had. He was remembering, too, that, aside from the law of sanctuary which governed the Temple of Eternal Light, neither Wu Ling nor the Chuen-to-yan had made the slightest effort to stay their departure.

And, above all, he was thinking of those oblique eyes of the Chuen-to-yan, hard and menacing as two black marbles. He could not believe that the Chuen-to-yan would accept defeat so easily as he had appeared to accept it.

And he knew Wu Ling would not. The Chuen-to-yan might not have ruled in the Temple of Eternal Light for a hundred and fifty years, as was reputed, but he was far, far older than Sir Gordon or Wu Ling, and Blake had seen enough of him to realise that he was possessed of a colossal intelligence. Blake was nervous —not in a physical sense, but keenly uneasy as to what subtle means the Chuen-to-yan would now employ to checkmate them. He was not at all ready to consider them as out of the wood, despite the optimism of Hsui-fsi, who, he reflected, was liable to lose sight of what was to come in his enjoyment of what he considered to be the best joke of many years.

Thus Blake was ruminating as they made their way unmolested through the Thieves' Market, and from there gained the Shameen, or foreign quarter.

"Nevertheless, I think it behoves us to be on guard," he insisted, after a long silence. "We are out of the temple, and we have come through the Thieves' Market unscathed. But we are not out of Canton yet, Sir Gordon."

The old man grew more composed. "You are right, Blake," he said. "I mustn't crow until we get clear. That old fiend of a Chuen-to-yan is capable of anything, but if the pigeon got away through the ventilating shaft, as it appeared, then there is no doubt that it would reach the cote at the house."

"If either Wu Ling or the Chuen-to-yan had revealed more anxiety, I should have felt easier," remarked Blake. "Still, I can't figure out what they could do. The pigeon had a good start, and they were still in the temple when we left. We know, too, that Tinker will handle things at the house as soon as the pigeon reached there, even if he is in bed with his wounds."

"There are plenty of things they could do without leaving the temple," rejoined Hsui-fsi in a graver tone. "I guess I have been ignoring that possibility, Blake. You make me feel uneasy. Let us make better speed."

They increased their pace then, and said no more until they turned into the wide street on which fronted the House of Two Hundred Intelligences, and which had a very large old garden at the rear which abutted on a similar garden at the back of the Eastern Hotel, where Tinker had put up on his arrival in Canton. It will be recalled, too, that both places were the private property of Hsui-fsi.

On approaching the house nothing appeared amiss. The great teak doors were closed fast, and there was only one light to be seen in a room which they knew to be the one now occupied by Tinker. But when Hsui-fsi had struck the heavy knocker half a dozen times without receiving any response, they turned and regarded each other uneasily.

"I don't like this, Blake," whispered Sir Gordon. "Something wrong. I wonder if Tinker has heard?"

"Keep at the knocker, Sir Gordon. I will throw some gravel up against the lad's window."

With that he stepped back into the road, and, picking up a handful of gravel, began to bombard the window above. He was still so employed, but without the slightest result so far as he could see, when a sound caused him to stride across to Sir Gordon. The latter was leaning against the door, listening intently, and he put his finger to his lips as Blake reached him. Blake, too, laid his ear against the teak, and then he caught the sound which had arrested Sir Gordon's knocking.

Inside there was a slow, dragging sound which seemed to be gradually approaching the door. It was as if some person, very old or crippled, were dragging himself along the stone passage in an effort to reach the door. The sound was accompanied by a sort of heavy wheezing, and as the pair outside listened they knew full well that something very serious indeed had happened at the House of Two

Hundred Intelligences, either while they had been in the temple, or since they had left it.

Sir Gordon pounded the knocker again, and, when the noise had died away inside the passage, they caught a choking sound, as if the person trying to reach them was making an effort to respond. They stood fretting impatiently until the sound stopped close inside the door. Then there was the rattle of a chain, and, a few moments later, they were able to push the door inwards.

The passage was lighted by a heavy grilled iron lantern, which, however, only gave out feeble rays. But they were strong enough to show them the figure of a human being lying prone on the stone at their feet, and, as they bent over, they recognised one of Sir Gordon's men, who had been left on guard when they departed for the temple.

That the man was in extremis was plain. But he was still conscious, and struggled frantically to communicate something to Sir Gordon.

Between them they lifted him up, but, as the light from the lantern fell on his features, they saw that he would never speak again, for a long, terrible gash had ripped his neck. How he had ever managed to drag himself along to the door was a mystery.

Blake slammed the door and hooked up the chain. Sir Gordon had eased the poor wretch to the stone.

"He is beyond help, Blake. We had better see what has happened."

Wait here, Sir Gordon. I want to run up to see if Tinker is in his room. Here, take this pistol in case you are attacked. I shall get another upstairs."

Without pausing for a reply Blake dashed through the passage and up the stairs to the passage leading to Tinker's room. The door was half-closed, but Blake kicked it open with a bang. Then, on the very threshold, he came to an abrupt halt. Tinker's bed was empty.

He turned and raced downstairs again, calling Tinker's name as he went. No answer came. Not one of the half-dozen faithful servants who had been left on guard was to be seen. With a word to Sir Gordon, Blake caught up a lantern and started on the run down the garden path towards the pagoda where he and Sir Gordon and Tinker had laid their plans against the enemy.

He reached the pagoda, but found it utterly empty.

Then he kept on until he had almost reached the little high-arched bridge which spanned the tiny brook that flowed through both gardens. And there he drew up with a gasp of consternation.

Strewn about like so many sleeping figures were at least a dozen Celestials, while in the very centre of them lay Tinker, his arms outflung and his face as white as frost under the rays of the lantern.

One second look Blake gave at the bodies on the ground, then he turned and raced back up the garden until he saw Sir Gordon coming towards him.

"Hurry!" he panted. "The place is a shambles!"

As Tinker drew nearer he was able to distinguish the strangers, and was now able to shoot without fear of hitting his own supporters. He promptly began firing, and the lad's sudden appearance with the automatic gave the invaders pause. (*Chapter 2.*)

IT did not need any more than that first glimpse to show Blake what good reason he had not to exult over the victory they had won at the Temple of Eternal Light until they were quite out of the wood.

And if he had had but the slightest inkling as to what was taking place at the House of Two Hundred Intelligences while he and Sir Gordon were making their way leisurely along on foot, he would have covered the intervening distance in about one-tenth the time it had taken.

It was not until some time later that Blake became convinced that in some way the Chuen-to-yan had managed to broadcast a message to his followers, even while they stood before him in the temple, and immediately following the departure of the homing pigeon taking with it the Ling-tse vase.

Just how it was done he could not guess, but no one realised better than Sexton Blake that it was comparatively simple to one of the devious mind and widespread power of the Chuen-to-yan. It was only from Tinker they were to get the true story of what had happened, and that only when Blake had carried the lad back to his bed-room, where it was more than an hour before he came round.

At first a deadly chill had gripped Blake's heart as he gazed upon the ghastly countenance of the lad as he lay almost in the grasp of death—for death it had been, sanguinary and terrible, for that dozen or more of Celestials who had battled there in the quiet garden. But, while a great bruise on Tinker's head showed how he had been struck down, his pulse still beat steadily, and the real danger was a fracture. The lad's natural endurance stood him in good stead that night, for a very little more and the weapon would have crashed through into the brain itself. And, according to what Tinker had to say, this is what happened:

During the last terrific efforts they had made to get possession of the Ling-tse vase Tinker had been badly beaten by the chief sacrificial priest of the temple, into which he had penetrated in pursuit of Wu Ling; and that, after being rescued from the Thieves' Market by Blake and Sir Gordon, he had had his wounds dressed and had been put to bed in the House of Two Hundred Intelligences while Blake and Hsui-fsi sallied forth to tackle Wu Ling and the Chuen-to-yan. Hsui-fsi had left half a dozen trustworthy guards on duty about the place, in case of emergencies, and, as far as Tinker knew, everything had been all right during the greater part of the evening.

Tinker had apparently been dozing, when suddenly he had been awakened by the sound of cries and the clash of arms beneath him. He had struggled out of bed, and, wounded though he was, had grabbed up his automatic and made his way along until he was on the balcony which overlooked the garden.

Although the night was murky and a heavy mist lay over the river, it was somewhat clearer in the more open quarter of the Shameen, in which the House of Two Hundred Intelligences was situated, and the garden itself was illuminated to a certain extent by several coloured paper lanterns which hung at different points throughout the garden. It was more by this light than anything else that Tinker was able to gain some idea of what was going on beneath.

Now, in order to gather a clear idea of just what was going on, it is necessary to explain that in the garden, just to the right-hand angle of the building, was a large dovecote in which Sir Gordon kept his homing pigeons, a thing that had been a hobby with him for many years.

It was while he and Blake had sat in the garden pagoda, discussing ways and means of outwitting Wu Ling and the Chuen-to-yan, that the idea had come to Hsui-fsi to utilise the services of one of the homing pigeons, if a way could be found. It was from that suggestion they had built up their scheme—which, of course, had depended for its success on certain conditions existing, or being made to exist, during their daring visit to the temple.

Despite the difficulty it had encountered immediately after Sir Gordon had released it, the homing instinct had triumphed, and the pigeon had found egress from the temple through the ancient ventilating-shaft and through the opening beneath the topmost pagoda, roof of the temple. From that it had been a simple flight to its cote in the garden of the House of Two Hundred Intelligences, where one of Hsui-fsi's servants had been waiting on duty for the moment when it should show up.

Tinker had been half asleep when the bird had come, and so had not witnessed its arrival. Nor did he know the exact moment when the Chinese servant secured the bird and released the little pouch containing the vase from beneath its wing.

It would have seemed that this clinched matters, and that at last, the Ling-tse vase was safe from either Wu Ling or the Chuen-to-yan. But a very few minutes after showed that the Chuen-to-yan had by no means accepted defeat so easily.

How he had managed to broadcast his warning will never be known, although later, Blake was inclined to lend some credence to Sir Gordon's theory that the warning had been sent out to one of the Chuen-to-yan adepts, who had probably been lying in wait for some days near the House of Two Hundred Intelligences, by telepathic means, which undoubtedly are extensively practised by the adepts of China, as well as of India and Thibet.

If that was not the case, it is difficult to understand how it was done, for it is a fact that during the time Blake and Sir Gordon were in the temple the Chuen-to-yan made no visible communication with anyone. But, however it was managed, it succeeded in its purpose, for even while the servant was at the cote a summons came on the great outer doors which shut the house off from the street.

Now, had it been a little later those who had been left on guard would have exercised more caution in opening the doors. But as it was known to all that the pigeon had arrived safely, and as they could not conceive how this could be known to any of the men serving Wu Ling or the Chuen-to-yan, it had apparently seemed reasonable to suppose that it must be Hsui-fsi and his guest who had managed to reach the house sooner than was expected.

The exact truth of that will never be known, either, for the whole guard was wiped out in the melee which followed. But the door was opened before a proper parley was held, with the result that a score of men poured through before Hsui-fsi's men could eject them. Then the melee had commenced, and it was the noise of this which roused Tinker.

As he reached the balcony, it was all too plain what had happened. The fight had been forced through the passage until it had debouched into the garden.

Over by the dovecote, Tinker caught sight of the man who had just released the vase from beneath the pigeon's wing. In a flash the lad grasped that the pigeon had returned, so he yelled a frantic warning to the servant telling him to make for the balcony, which they might be able to hold.

A few seconds before, there would have been time for this, but now it was too late, and as the man was spied by one of the invaders there was a great shout raised, and several of them took after him. He turned and dashed down the garden path, apparently with the intention of trying to shake them off in the dark bypaths, or else to reach the other garden which abutted beyond at the back of the Eastern Hotel.

Tinker saw that, with Hsui-fsi's men outnumbered almost two to one by the invaders, only a herculean effort could save the situation. Despite his own physical weakness, he somehow managed to get down the stairs and into the garden.

By now the chase had almost disappeared along the path that led to the pagoda, but the racket was yet sufficient to tell the lad that the melee still raged. Tinker went staggering along in that direction until he saw, just beneath one of the coloured lights close to the pagoda, a mass of men. He broke into a feeble trot, for at the distance he dared not shoot for fear of hitting one of his own supporters. But as he drew closer he was able to distinguish the strangers, and promptly began firing.

Tinkers sudden appearance with the deadly automatic gave the invaders pause for a moment, and, taking advantage of this, the man who had possession of the vase turned and raced along towards the bridge which spanned the little stream.

Tinker gave a shout to spur him on, but the next second he lost sight of the fugitive as the struggle recommenced. By one accord, both defenders and invaders seemed to give towards the bridge, and, as Tinker hurled himself into the thick of it, clubbing his now empty automatic, he found himself carried along in the press.

Then things became so confused to the lad that he scarcely knew what was happening. He was needing all his will power to keep control of his swimming senses, yet he was vaguely aware that, while he was struggling in a hand-to-hand battle with a Celestial, who was making frantic efforts to knife him, they were swept along by the mess until those in the rear were actually on the near end of the bridge.

He caught a flash then as the one for whose safety they were fighting broke clear again, and made for the stream. As the others took after, Tinker saw the fugitive disappear round a thick, bushy tree, which he had noticed before as he crossed the bridge. Then, almost immediately after, there came a long-drawn wail, followed by a sudden silence.

"They've got him!" panted the lad as he forced a way through.

"By heavens, they will get the vase!"

At this thought he fell savagely upon the man nearest him, shouting as he did so to the few surviving defenders to renew the struggle. Once more the melee rose to a furious pitch, and then, just as Tinker thought he could make his way through, something hit him on the head, and he went down as if a thunderbolt had struck him. What happened after that he did not know, nor did Blake and Hsui-fsi ever find out.

But had they been there they would have seen three of the fiends hurl themselves upon the luckless fugitive. As if a new spirit had entered into them, the remaining defenders once more renewed the battle; and from that it was a vicious slaughter, raging about beneath the coloured lanterns, and making the scene a wild, mad whirl of insane marionettes, such as one could only picture in the crazy confusion of a nightmare. One by one they went down, wounded, gasping, but still thrusting outwards and upwards with those vicious knives, until the last pair fell weakly to one side, made one final effort to deliver the coup de grace, then collapsed in one motionless mound.

And thus they lay, until the silence of that shambles was shattered by the hollow echo of the great iron knocker on the doors which gave on to the street. From the heap of dead and dying, one being dragged himself slowly along towards the house, and, as the knocking still resounded, he managed to reach the door and drag off the chain. But that was all; and, as his master and Sexton Blake came in his loyal spirit fluttered away.

It is little wonder, therefore, that Sexton Blake was aghast at the spectacle. But with Blake all things were thrust aside until he had ascertained Tinker's exact condition.

With extraordinary gentleness, he lifted the lad in his arms and carried him back to his room. There he re-dressed the wounds which had been caused by the lash in the temple, after which he gave his attention to the lad's head. It had been a wicked blow, and, a little more straight in direction, it would have have cracked the skull like an eggshell. But, although the contusion was severe, the bone itself did not appear to be seriously injured; and when, after a strenuous hour, Tinker finally regained consciousness, Blake heaved a mighty sigh of relief.

It went against the grain to permit the lad to talk then, but by now it was plain that the vase must have been the reason for the raid, and it was of the utmost urgency that they should find out as quickly as possible just what had occurred, or, at least, as much as Tinker could tell them.

As soon as they grasped its import both Blake and Sir Gordon made for the garden, and with the aid of electric torches, began their gruesome search.

They found the body of the Celestial who had fled with the vase lying just where he had been murdered behind the great bush.

Had his murderers secured the vase? If so, then it ought to be found, for none could have fled from the scene of that terrible struggle. The door, which they had found chained on the inside, was sufficient proof of that.

But, though they went about their gruesome task with all the method which Sexton Blake knew so well how to employ, the rising sun found them still at work with no success. As they finished with the last prone form, Blake paused for a moment.

"With daylight we can get to work on the ground," he said wearily. "It must be here somewhere. None could have got away, and we know that the pigeon arrived safely. Tinker saw sufficient to be certain of that."

"It must be about the ground or among these bushes," responded Sir Gordon, who, despite his nearly fourscore years and ten, had insisted on helping Blake throughout the long night. "And if it is here, it must be found. I'll have fifty men here in half an hour, and we will comb every inch of the place."

Blake lighted a cigarette, and strolled up on to the little bridge to wait for Sir Gordon's return. From where he stood he could look down on the last scene of the fight, and could visualise just how the murder of the Celestial, who had fled with the precious vase, had taken place.

The huge bush stood out plainly now in the misty dawn, and Blake saw that it was of the chen-tok or giant Yang-tse bean species. From its branches hung thick clusters of the giant bean, whose pods contain the kernels so rich in oil, and which are such a valuable item of food value in the interior of China. Not one was less than eight inches, and some must have measured almost a foot in length, while in thickness a few ran as thick as a man's wrist.

Blake noted casually that they had evidently reached maturity, for as the bushes stirred gently in the light breeze the drying pods rustled and crackled, while a few which were fully ripe were detached by the movement and fell into the stream to go sailing gaily away like miniature boats.

How little did Sexton Blake realise, as he idly watched them, that in this phenomenon of Nature lay the secret of the fate of the Ling-tse vase, which was to defy solution that day!

But, if Blake had only known all the details of what had occurred behind that bush of death, he would have realised how utterly abortive was to be their search of the garden. But none had seen the act which had altered the whole course of events, and which, while placing the precious vase out of reach of either Wu Ling or the Chuen-to-yan for the time being, was to start it on a new career that was to continue the trail of blood and death which it had blazed.

Like a hare, the unfortunate victim who had fled for safety, had dashed behind the chen-tok bush, his pursuers close at his heels. In rounding the bush, his idea had been to make across the brook and try to shake off the enemy among the more remote paths which he knew so well.

But he was pressed too closely; yet even in that moment so fraught with peril, his only thought had been the safety of the sacred prize which he bore. And it was in the very act of passing behind the bush —it was even at the moment when those murderous knives were flashing behind him —that his swinging hand had encountered a cluster of the giant bean-pods.

The touch was dry and hard, and he knew that a faint pressure would be sufficient to open the longitudinal jointure of the pod.

At the very moment when the foremost of his pursuers flung himself upon him, the doomed man succeeded in grasping one of the pods. He went crashing down, but his will power fought to check that last plunge of his senses into the abyss of darkness until he had accomplished his task.

And this he did.

While those vicious blades were still slashing at him, he managed to press the pod apart, and into the aperture he slipped the little vase. But as the last fury of the murderers struck him, he crashed forward, tearing the cluster of pods from the bunch as he went down. Nor did anyone see the beans scatter upon the surface of the little brook, and go sailing away towards the great yellow current which was blanketed by the heavy night mist.

That was what neither Blake nor Sir Gordon knew; that was what Tinker could not tell them. That was why, after a solid three days of fruitless labour, when every blade of grass had been examined, they were forced to abandon their efforts, completely at a loss to understand what had become of the Ling-tse vase.

And it was with a feeling of savage disappointment that, at the end of that time, Blake made his arrangements to return to London, his only consolation being that, as far as they could discover, both Wu Ling and the Chuen-to-yan were as much in the dark as they. Sir Gordon was to remain behind at the House of Two Hundred Intelligences in order to pursue a last desperate search for the vase.

Thus it was that, with Tinker once more able to get about, Blake and the lad took the night boat for Hong Kong, in order to catch the Canadian-Pacific liner for Vancouver.

THE THIRD CHAPTER. *Mr. Carter of London, has an Agreeable Surprise.*

IN his capacity as buyer for his own small antique shop in London, Mr. Bertram Carter was almost an annual visitor to the China coast, with the exception of a more extended journey every three or four years to India and Burmah.

About fifty years of age, but, owing to his somewhat spare figure, stooped shoulders, and one cross-eye, he looked nearer sixty; and, at first glance, the casual observer would have put him down as possessing a rather forbidding personality.

On the contrary, however, he was a most genial soul, full of any number of droll yarns, which he had picked up during many years of world travel, an excellent bridge player, and extremely generous, which is all that one can very well ask in a travelling acquaintance.

While indulging his fancy over pretty well the whole range of Japanese and Chinese antiques, his real speciality was ceramics, of which he was considered by European and American authorities as a connoisseur, and on which, indeed, he had at one time written a most erudite monograph.

And it was while on one of his periodical visits to Canton, where he had made several very satisfactory purchases, that his enthusiasm for his favourite merchandise was to make him a cog in one of the biggest battle of wits which had ever gone on behind the yellow screen of Chinese intrigue.

On a certain morning following a night when it had been rumoured throughout the Shameen quarter that Dr. Sun-Yat-Sen had once more been driven to take refuge on a gunboat in the river, due to a night attack by one of the recalcitrant generals who are continually hovering on the outskirts trying to seize some need of power during the general confusion in South China, Mr. Carter heaved a sigh of satisfaction as he stepped aboard the river steamer Canton to proceed to Hong Kong, where it was his intention to embark by a P. and O. steamer for Colombo, where he would tranship to the Bibby boat, for London.

He heaved a sigh of relief, it may be explained, for the reason that, once before he had had an experience of a night attack on Canton, and had seen a little of the looting which had followed. But the gentleman would have been much less perturbed if he had known

17

that the rumours circulating in the Shameen were not quite correct.

There had been a good deal of trouble during the night, but the fighting had had nothing to do with the figurehead president of the so-called republic of South China or one of the recalcitrant generals.

It had been entirely an inter-tong affair, staged in the notorious Thieves' Market, in which three of the most powerful tongs in China had been engaged, and in which that of the Three Feathers, under the leadership of a certain very powerful and mysterious person, known in China as Hsui-fsi, assisted by another person, who seemed to be a mandarin of the purple button, but who was, in reality, none other than Sexton Blake, the famous London criminologist, had given a severe drubbing to the tong known as the Brotherhood of the Yellow Beetle, and another, known as the Black Valley Tong, which was under the direct control of the powerful Chuen-to-yan, of the Temple of Eternal Light, and thus the supreme head of all the Buddhists in China.

It had been a most sanguinary affair, followed by certain isolated clashes later the same night. But there had been no danger of any looting in the Shameen quarter, and hence Mr. Carter's nervousness was unjustified.

However, there was little chance of the truth leaking through to a European traveller, so the antique dealer was well content when, at last, he found himself safe on board the Canton, with the only probable danger to anticipate between Canton and Hong Kong —the junk pirates off Macao. For these pests have multiplied in an extraordinary fashion during the last five years, and, in their increased daring, are a real danger to small coastwise traffic.

Somewhat to his disappointment, Mr. Carter found himself, with one exception, the only European passenger on board, and, as this exception was obviously one of the numerous soldiers of fortune to be found all up and down the coast, the antique dealer took good care to shun him. He had met up with gentlemen of that ilk before, and, during his first visit to China, had parted with a nice little round sum of cash in return for a considerable amount of unwanted experience.

Therefore, after seeing his numerous cases safely stowed away, Carter amused himself by watching the teeming sampan and junk life of the river until the steamer got under way. He put in half an hour in the cubby-hole, which, with an entire lack of humorous intent, was called the European saloon; but the strength of the odour given off by a very stout Eurasian, who had insisted on European accommodation, drove him back to the deck.

In order to avoid the necessity for staving off any attempt at approach on the part of the adventurer, he made his way forward to watch a game of fan-tan, which had already started on the Chinese deck. So interested did he become in this that he finally determined to take a hand in the fun.

Although he played only mildly, he found, considerably to his surprise, that, at the end of a couple of hours or so, he had contributed a surprising number of Hong Kong dollars to the needs of the wily old Celestial who was running the game, and, somewhat annoyed with himself, he returned to the deck above, never dreaming that, at that very moment, Fate was sweeping towards him on the yellow current of the river an object which was to carry him into the tortuous course of affairs which were to spell his doom.

It was just after he had reached the upper deck, and had strolled aft that Carter paused to watch a Chinese deckhand dragging up water from the river in an ordinary galvanised pail, to the handle of which a rope had been tied. Apparently the man had some reluctant intention of sluicing the water along the deck, in order to flush out the scuppers; but what he was only succeeding in doing was to precipitate most of the water over the edge of the half deck on to the heads of some luckless deck passengers who were just beneath.

After he had watched this useless waste of effort for a few minutes, the antique dealer was about to move away when, as the man drew up another pail, he saw floating in the water a gigantic pod, which looked like nothing more nor less than a bean pod of a species unknown in Europe.

Out of sheer curiosity he signed to the man to wait, and, bending over, took out the pod. The man watched him with an impersonal, indulgent Chinese grin.

Turning, Carter walked along the deck, endeavouring as he did so to press open the longitudinal jointure of the pod, in order to discover what sort of bean this strange sort of pod produced. He had never heard of, or seen, the giant Yang-tse bean, and hence did not know that what he held was a very ordinary product of the interior.

From the colour of the outside shell it was plain that the pod had been practically dry and mature when it had fallen into the water, but since then the shell had become saturated, with the result that it had swollen somewhat, and, in doing so, had tightened the jointure.

But after a few clumsy efforts the antique dealer succeeded in pressing it apart, and a second later he stood staring in dumbfounded amazement at the strangest bean that had ever come from a pod, and which was now lying in the palm of his hand.

Bertram Carter wasn't very well versed in the real hidden mysteries of China, but he had come upon quite sufficient during his several visits to Canton, and other cities along the coast, to realise that there were many, many things of which the outside world did not even guess.

And, somehow, instinct told him that this strange object, which had been borne along on the yellow current, inside the giant pod, must be connected in some way with those dark movements, the force of which he had vaguely felt.

It was that instinct which caused his fingers to close over the palm of his hand, even as his first startled glance told him that what he held was a small, but exquisitely beautiful, example of ancient Chinese ceramics such as he had never come upon before.

His collector's soul rejoiced gleefully at such a find, and now his one desire was to get away somewhere by himself, in order to endeavour to examine his find safely, and to place the period to which it must belong. Bertram Carter, connoisseur though he was, had never heard of the jealously guarded, and very sacred, Ling-tse vase; otherwise, his first glimpse would have told him that what he held was either that wondrous object or a faultless copy.

He had, as a matter of course, taken a small cabin, but had simply placed his hand luggage there with no intention of occupying it, as it was, if anything, slightly more malodorous than the "saloon."

But now he sought its privacy, and he set himself to make a close examination of the vase. When he had finished his wondering scrutiny of the extraordinary maze of cabalistic symbols which decorated it inside and out, he knew beyond any further doubt that, whatever its origin, it was unquestionably the most valuable ceramic object he had ever seen or heard of.

He thought, with a good deal of inward satisfaction, of the stir such a find would create among the collectors of Europe and America; and he hadn't any doubt but that he would realise a very substantial price, which, considering it hadn't cost him a single tael, looked like a pretty good piece of business.

So it was with no little satisfaction he finally locked it away and returned to the deck.

The Canton docked at Kowloon that same evening, and Mr. Bertram Carter betook himself and his luggage across on the ferry, and on to the Hong-Kong Hotel. His first care, after securing his room, was to ascertain at what time the P. & O. boat would sail for Singapore.

He found that this was to be early the following evening, which gave him a welcome twenty-four hours in Hong Kong, as, after his usual custom, he would dispatch to his London address, by registered parcel-post, a good many of his smaller, and most valuable, purchases, in case he should decide later to remain over a week or so in Ceylon.

That little duty attended to, the antique dealer made for the bar, where, to his pleasure, he immediately ran into a quartette of American tourists with whom he had travelled down from Yokohama. After greetings had been exchanged he drew up a chair, and the usual round of "stingahs" and exchange of experiences started.

It appeared that the Americans had been across to Macao, the very old and curious outpost which Portugal still maintains on the China Coast, and where there exists an Eastern gambling casino which is even more interesting than that at Monte Carlo. Their play had not been any too profitable, and when he had heard their story, the antique dealer related his own experience with fan-tan on the way down from Hong Kong.

"But that isn't the half of what I struck," he added, with a screwing up of his cross-eye, which the Americans now knew to be meant for a smile. "I had the biggest piece of luck that ever happened to me since I have been a collector of antiques."

A chorus of questions at once assailed him, for it was plain the Englishman was not joking, and, pluming himself considerably, Carter related just what had happened. On the conclusion of his yarn the chorus that had been one of credulous interest, now changed to hilarious incredulity, but it gradually died away when it was evident that the dealer was not joking.

"I give you my word it is the truth— every word," he protested. "And just to prove it to you, I will show you the vase. You wait here. I shall not be more than a few moments."

With that he jumped up and left the bar; nor did he or the other four take note of the fact that all during the recital a Chinese "boy" had been hovering not far away, and now began to busy himself still closer to the table at which Carter had been sitting.

In less than five minutes the antique dealer was back, and, as he sat down, he took from his pocket the little vase which he had found in such strange fashion. While none of the quartette was an expert in such matters, it didn't need that to realise that the tiny object was a very fine piece of work, and, as it was passed round, the exclamations of admiration at its beauty were perfectly sincere.

They were too engrossed to notice that the Chinese "boy" had moved over until he could see without difficulty what it was, nor did they witness the very slight lowering of the heavy lids as he turned away and shuffled towards the door. And less than ten minutes later a telegram was on its way to the Chuen-to-yan of the Temple of Eternal Light in Canton.

The antiquarian kept his newest treasure in his pocket while he dined with the Americans, and, on mounting to his room, locked it up again with his other purchases. Little would that have availed him, however, were it not that the Celestial who had sent the message to the Chuen-to-yan was waiting for instructions. He knew that, if he was right, and it was indeed the sacred Ling-tse vase which he had seen, those instructions would not be long in coming, and that they would be that he was to secure the vase at any cost.

Therefore, although he did not know it, the antique dealer was kept under a constant surveillance by watchful eyes while he slept, quite in ignorance of the yellow whirlpool that was seething about him.

The following morning Carter busied himself with packing the few smaller objects among his purchases which he intended to despatch by registered parcel-post to London. When this was completed he took the box downstairs, and along to the shipping agency, whose office was in one corner of the hotel. Finishing his business there, he went in to tiffin, and in the afternoon joined his American acquaintances in an expedition to the Peak.

It was just after five o'clock when they returned, so, since Carter wished to be aboard before seven, he took tea hurriedly, then made his preparations to depart. When his luggage was all collected, a Chinese "boy" went to get him a car to take him along to the dock, where the steam launch was waiting.

It was just dusk as he stepped out of the hotel, and he paid little attention to the fact that two Celestials were standing by the door of the closed motor, accidentally, or otherwise, cutting off a view of the interior. Carter pushed past them, and, after giving his destination to the driver —also a Celestial —he stepped in.

It was only then he noticed, with some surprise, that the car already had an occupant.

Thinking there had been some mistake, he muttered something and started to back out, but at that moment a heavy push came from behind, and he was sent sprawling into the vehicle.

His mouth opened to utter an amazed protest, but before a single syllable could make itself audible a pair of sinewy hands reached down and gripped him like a vice by the throat, and at the same instant the car began to move.

SEXTON BLAKE and Tinker delayed their departure Canton until the last possible moment in order to give Tinker's wounds every chance to heal before the fatigue of travelling, for it became more and more apparent to Blake's searching eyes that the lad's condition was by no means as trivial as Tinker would have had him believe.

By telegraphing to Hong Kong, Blake discovered that the Canadian Pacific liner was scheduled to sail for Vancouver at eight o'clock in the morning, so he laid his plans accordingly.

They left Canton on the night boat, which got away about six in the evening, with the result that they reached Hong Kong at six the following morning —just in time to trans-ship direct from the Canton boat to the liner, which rode at anchor out in the fairway at one of the giant mooring-buoys.

Thus it was that they did not land in the port itself, and hence the reason they heard nothing of the murder of an Englishman which had taken place two nights before and which had stirred up considerable sensation in the place.

The liner sailed promptly on time, and, after a breakfast which tasted more than appetising after the fare in Canton, Blake forced Tinker to stretch out in a long deck-chair while he went below to see after their unpacking. As neither of them was very keen just then to mix to any great extent in the life aboard ship, they kept pretty much to themselves in the secluded corner which Blake had secured for their chairs, and for the first three days out about the only contact they had with any of their fellow-passengers was to nod a brief greeting to those who sat at the same table.

But on the third day Blake, who was feeling in a better frame of mind owing to the rapidity with which Tinker was picking up under the stimulating sea air, betook himself along to the smoking-saloon, with the object of sitting in at a game of bridge if there should be a vacancy.

On arriving there, a rapid survey showed him that for the time being he would have to wait, as every table filled, so he called the steward, and after ordering a drink settled down in one corner under an electric fan.

Beyond the captain and chief officer, with whom he had travelled before, there was no one on board whom Blake knew; but it was evident that his identity had leaked out, for as he walked along the deck he noticed signs that the other passengers were speaking about him to one another, and now, as his glance roved about the smoking-saloon, he saw, with a touch of inward amusement, that a group of American tourists were undoubtedly discussing him.

As that was nothing new to Blake, he paid no further attention, but confined himself to his drink, until he suddenly became aware that someone was standing in front of him, undoubtedly addressing him in a strong American accent.

"Excuse me, sir," the man was saying, "but am I correctly informed that you are Mr. Sexton Blake, the famous London criminologist?"

Blake smiled faintly.

"I am Sexton Blake and I am a criminologist." he responded civilly. "As to the rest of the description, I am afraid I can hardly presume to answer."

"I guess you don't have to, Mr. Blake!" rejoined the other. "Your name is just as familiar to us in America as it is in Europe. I beg your pardon for addressing you, but there is something my friends and I want to ask you since you also came aboard at Hong Kong. My name is Fenton —James K. Fenton, of the Fenton Cement Company of San Francisco. But I guess, maybe, you have never heard of me?"

"Why, yes, Mr. Fenton, I have." answered Blake pleasantly. "Let me see, was not your firm responsible for some of the first cement ships built during the war?"

"You hit it first shot, Mr. Blake! But concrete ships, I am sorry to say, didn't quite prove out as big a thing as we thought they would. But now, if you don't mind, I'll just ask you your opinion about what I and my friends have been discussing. I am not seeking professional advice."

"All right. If you will sit down I shall do my best to answer what you wish to ask me."

"Thank you. It's about this murder in Hong Kong, Mr. Blake. We want to know what you think about it. It upset us quite a good bit, I can tell you since we travelled down from Yokohama with the victim and were with him up to a short time before he was murdered. We have been wondering what theory you formed about it."

Blake was gazing at his interlocutor blankly.

"Murder? I don't quite understand, Mr. Fenton. I know of no

murder in Hong Kong. When did it take place? And who was the victim?"

"Well, I'm darned! Do you mean to say you have heard nothing of the murder of an Englishman two nights ago —an antique dealer by the name of Carter?"

"Not a word. I have been in Canton on business, and came down with my assistant only the night before this ship was due to sail. We went straight on board from the river-boat. That is probably why I heard nothing. You say this murder took place two nights ago?"

"Yes. A most mysterious affair."

"You mentioned that the victim was an antique-dealer and that his name was Carter. I wonder if it could, by any chance, be Bertram Carter —a rather elderly man, with a cast in one eye?"

"The very man! Did you know him?"

"Why, not particularly well. But I have purchased a few things from him in London, and on one occasion I met him on the China coast. It was his custom, I understand, to come out East each year to buy new stock."

"That is the very man. Well, if you haven't heard about it I will tell you, if you would like to hear it."

"Most assuredly! I am shocked at the news!"

"Nobody seems able to arrive at a motive. And there is a good deal of mystery attached to it. As I said, we came down with Carter from Yokohama, and all of us left the steamer at Hong Kong; but while he went up to Canton to buy some antiques, we went across to Macao. On our return to Hong Kong we ran into Carter again, and found him in high spirits over what, he figured, was the greatest piece of luck that had happened to him during the whole of his business career. It was a darned curious thing, too. But I'll tell you about it later."

"Why not now?" interrupted Blake. "Who knows, it may have some bearing on the mystery."

"I guess not; but I'll explain. Carter was coming down from Canton, and was mooching about the deck with nothing to do, when he stopped to watch a Chinese deck-hand drawing up water in a pail to douse over the deck. In one of these pails of water Carter noticed floating a bean of some sort, and, because it was the largest of its kind he had ever seen, he reached over and took it out. He was walking along the deck, pressing it open to see what sort of a bean could be inside such a pod, when suddenly there popped out into his hand a very small but wonderfully made vase, which he was positive was of great antiquity. He — What's that, Mr. Blake?"

"Nothing, Mr. Fenton. An exclamation of amazement only. Please go on. I find the story extremely interesting."

"Oh, you probably think it is a yarn which Carter was spinning to pull our legs; but I can assure you, Mr. Blake, it was the truth, for he showed us the vase, and, believe me, it was a little beauty!"

"It couldn't have been very large, to be found inside the pod of which you speak. I take it the pod must have been one of the giant Yang tse beans which are common in the interior of China. They run in length from seven or eight inches to a foot, or even more."

"I guess it must have been one of those, then. Anyway, the vase wasn't very big—about as big as, let me see —"

"The end of your thumb, say? Or perhaps a lady's thimble?"

"You've hit it, Mr. Blake —just about the size of a lady's thimble. Well, that's the story of the vase. It sounds queer, but is quite true. But to get back to the murder. The afternoon before he sailed, Carter went up to the Peak with us, and, afterwards, we all had tea together. We saw him pass out a few minutes later on his way to the jetty.

"And that's the last we did see of him or hear of him; in fact, until his body was fished out of the harbour the next morning. He had been murdered— strangled with a cord that had cut very deeply into his neck. But when it happened, where it was done, how it could have been brought off in the short distance between the hotel and the jetty, what the motive was, is all a mystery.

"The Hong Kong police, however, are of the opinion that he was killed for his luggage, because not a single piece has been traced. Nor have they been able to trace the motor-car in which he drove away from the hotel. Now you, as a professional criminologist, ought to be able to deduce things from that case which would miss the ordinary layman, and that is why we would like to know what you think of it. Not that there's much chance of running down the Chinese devils who did it, though."

Blake lighted a fresh cigarette and motioned for the steward to bring two more drinks. He did not speak until the tumblers had been set before them; then he said:

"It is a very different thing, Mr. Fenton, to make any attempt at sound deduction purely from the relation of a crime. In my profession it is of the greatest importance that investigations should be made on the scene. It is usually there that the little clues, which mean so much, are to be found. However, let us just take this and analyse it a little. Firstly, I think you said the murder took place two nights ago?"

"That is so."

"Um! Well, I was in Canton that night."

But Blake did not add that he was thinking privately that it must have been just two nights after the massacre in the garden of the House of Two Hundred Intelligences. Nor did he make any mention of the fact that he had also taken note that, according to what the American had said, the antique dealer must have left Canton the morning following that trouble. Which meant that the finding of the giant pod, which had been fished up from the yellow current, must have been some sixteen or eighteen hours after the melee.

Or, in other words, just the length of time it would take for a light, floating substance to reach the river by way of the tiny brook which flowed through the Shameen, and be carried some miles down by the current.

It wasn't much in itself, but the fact that a tiny vase had been found under such extraordinary circumstances, the certainty that it could not have found its way inside that pod without human aid, and, above all, Blake's recollection that the servant who had tried to carry it to safety had been murdered at the very base of a giant Yang-tse bean-bush, which grew close to the edge of the stream, were altogether sufficient to quicken his pulse appreciably.

Half an hour before he had been convinced that the Ling-tse vase was gone for ever.

Now —well, it was too soon yet to form any definite opinion; but if this extraordinary tale he had just been listening to was true, then anything might be possible.

And Blake was beginning to think he knew how it might have occurred. But he showed nothing of this to the American. He was only anxious now to get all the facts out of him which he could.

"Of course, you know," he proceeded conversationally, "there are a good many queer things about China. It is not impossible that among his purchases in Canton, Mr. Carter happened upon something which should not have been taken out of the country. That would be one sufficient motive for certain Celestials to follow him and kill him.

Again, he may have unwittingly incurred the enmity of some one of the numerous tongs existing there.

"As you know, Mr. Fenton, both your race and my own, are, at times, liable to give offence to Eastern peoples without intending to do so. It is so easy for the Briton or the American to ride roughshod over some of their pet prejudices, which, while they mean nothing to us, are sacred to the Easterner."

"I get you there, Mr. Blake," grinned the American. "I guess I have offended that way myself."

"Well, that is another possible motive. Then, again, owing to the fact that it would be well known that Mr. Carter usually made valuable purchases when he came to Canton, the whole thing may have been simply a piece of planned banditry, which it was found impossible to bring off before the night he was leaving Hong Kong. I have seen a good many things happen in that port, and it would not be at all difficult to achieve such a thing between the hotel and the jetty.

"For instance, Mr. Fenton, recalling a not very different incident, which occurred some time ago there, I could make a fairly reasonable guess that when Mr. Carter stepped into the car, which was to take him to the jetty, he found that it was already occupied, and, before he could discover the reason, he was hauled inside, and rendered unconscious by a powerful drug, without a chance to defend himself. Something along those lines, I should say.

"Then, of course, instead of driving to the jetty, the car would simply head for the heart of the lower bazaar or along the harbour road to some quiet spot on the outskirts, where it would not be difficult to complete the work. The luggage would be looted, the actual bags and boxes destroyed, the victim dropped into the harbour, and the loot itself passed rapidly through a dozen different hands in the bazaar. To trace it would be practically hopeless.

"In all probability, it is either in Canton by now, or on its way to some other spot—Suchow or Swatow. I am afraid that is the best I can do in regard to a theory, and it seems it is about the one on which the Hong Kong police are working."

"I suppose it is just a common case of murder, with robbery the motive, Mr. Blake, but it was sure tough luck on the old man! He was a queer duck, but a very agreeable person when you got to know him, and we were more than cut up at the news, I can tell you. I hope you don't mind my approaching you as I did. Perhaps you would care to join in a rubber this evening?"

"I don't mind in the least; and I shall be happy to take a hand this evening. And now, if you will excuse me, I shall go along to see how my assistant is getting on. He was rather injured in Canton."

The American uttered a few words of sympathy, after which Blake nodded pleasantly and left the saloon. But, as he came up the deck, there was a purpose in his stride and a kindling light in his eye that told Tinker something had surely happened to stir his master more than any bridge hand could have stirred him. He wasn't long in discovering what it was. As Blake dropped into the deck-chair beside him, he brought his fist down on the arm and said in low, tense tunes:

"Listen, my lad, while I put a theory before you.

"Do you remember that just on the bank of the brook, close to where you were knocked unconscious in the garden that night, and behind which Hsui-fsi's man was killed, was a large Yang-tse bean-bush?"

"Yes, sir, of course," answered Tinker, in some surprise. "What about it?"

"Listen then. When the invaders succeeded in getting into the place, Hsui-fsi's servant had just secured the Ling-tse vase from the carrier-pigeon. As the fight commenced, he tried to getaway down the garden to a place of safety, after failing to reach the balcony where you were standing. But he was quickly overtaken; and, until you arrived on the scene, it looked hopeless for him. Your arrival, however, gave him another chance, which he took.

"He managed to get as far as the Yang-tse bean-bush, where he was again overtaken, and, this time, killed.

"You were unconscious, and could not see what was taking place. But, supposing, as the man went down, he felt his hand strike against a cluster of the giant-beans? I was standing on the little bridge at sunrise the next morning, and I recall seeing this bush.

"It was packed with matured pods, which were dry enough to rustle in the morning' breeze, and indeed, some were sufficiently ripe to fall off and float down on the current. Well, supposing this man should get a sudden inspiration; should press open one of those dry pods almost at the very moment when he was about to be knifed, and should succeed in slipping the vase inside?

"It's feasible enough. The pods are tough, and the jointure would quickly close again after the pressure had been released. Then go a step farther, and picture that either the jerk he gave it, or the fact that it was ready to fall, caused it to drop into the stream. We know that stream empties into the river, and thus, if a pod struck no obstruction, it would find its way into the river, and eventually out to sea."

Tinker grinned as Blake paused.

"Gee, guv'nor, that's pretty good. You have only been gone half an hour, too. It must be pretty good stuff they sell in the smoking saloon on this boat."

Blake nodded as he lit a cigarette.

"I am not surprised that you think I am trying to entertain you with a cooked-up theory, my lad. But wait; you haven't heard the half of it yet. Now, then, you know, of course, that there is a morning boat down from Canton to Hong Kong as well as an evening boat. Very well, let us say our giant pod reached the river during the early hours of the morning —anything between three and five. It would then have a couple of hours or so to drift down on the current before that morning boat started.

"Now, picture yourself on board idling about. We will say that you paused on the deck to watch a deckhand drew up a bucket of water, and in this you saw a giant pod, such as you had never seen before. Being mildly interested you would, very naturally, pick it out to examine it.

"Well, my lad, what would yon think if, on pressing it apart, a small vase, about the size of a woman's thimble, dropped into your hand?"

"I'd think I was back in the Thieves' Market, guv'nor. Still, I don't know, that might happen in China; but don't let me stop you. I didn't know you went in for fiction stories. I suppose you have thought out a nice finish to the plot?"

Blake laughed softly.

"Yes. This is it. If you were an antiquarian you would be highly interested at such a find, wouldn't you? And, on making a detailed examination, you would know, if you were an expert, that the vase was one of considerable antiquity and great value, even if you did not know anything about the Ling-tse vase. Now then, supposing it were the Ling-tse vase, and, on your arrival in Hong Kong, you felt so exultant about your find that you confided it publicly to some travelling acquaintances, afterwards showing them the vase in proof of your story?

"All right. The following night you are due to leave Hong Kong. You say good-bye to your friends. You enter a car waiting to take you to the jetty. You never reach the jetty. Nothing more is seen or heard of you until your body is fished out of the harbour the following morning with a strangling cord still about the neck, and not a trace of your luggage or the car in which you drove away is to be found.

"What would you say to that?"

"I'd say it was a pretty slick story, guv'nor. If the Ling-tse vase was found in that way there would be plenty of Chinks to do in the man who found it. All right for fiction, of course; but how could it get into the pod, and, then, how was it fished up in the bucket?"

"Just as I have told you, my lad —it actually occurred. How the vase got into the pod we can only guess. But at the time of leaving Canton we know, for a fact, that neither Wu Ling nor the Chuen-to-yan was in possession of it, and, of course, all our efforts to find it in the garden failed. Then, what did become of it?

"We know that every man who fought in the garden that night was killed. It was one of the worst tong battles I have ever come up against. It was fought with a fury which asked and gave no quarter. We are fairly certain that you are the only person who survived it.

"Very well. That being so, the vase should have been there, when Sir Gordon and I returned. But it wasn't. We didn't miss a single blade of grass. Then why isn't it a tenable theory that it was placed in the pod as a last desperate resource on the part of Hsui-fsi's servant?"

"That seems sound enough, guv'nor," admitted Tinker; "but the other —"

"The other, my lad, is the one part about the whole story that is not theory. It is fact, every item of it."

"Good heavens, guv'nor! Then you haven't been making up a story to amuse me?"

"Not in the least. I have just heard the whole story in the smoking saloon. I will give you the names and other details."

With that Blake related all that the American had told him. Tinker, who knew now that Blake was in deadly earnest, sat listening in dumbfounded amazement until he had finished. Then he said:

"But what can you do, guv'nor? Here we are three days out, and not a stop between here and Vancouver."

"We have the wireless, my lad, and Sir Gordon Saddler is still in Canton. I shall wireless him the whole story, and get the machinery started which he controls. It may be too late —probably is. For if they found the Ling-tse vase in Carter's luggage, then it must by now be in the possession of either Wu Ling or the Chuen-to-yan.

"But we will not give up trying until Hsui-fsi tells us this is so. To think that this should happen on the very eve of our departure! To think we were at Hong Kong; and didn't hear a word of the affair! If ever I believed in Lady Luck, I should say that she has been making fair sport of us ever since we tackled this infernal business."

With that Blake gave an angry thump on the arm of his chair, then he sprang to his feet, and went off to make out his code wireless message to Hsui-fsi, Mystery Man of 'Frisco, and the Englishman who had become Chinese.

NEEDLESS to say, Blake's message to Sir Gordon was a very voluminous affair, which was destined to give that aged individual a considerable shock.

But if Blake hoped for any satisfactory news while on the high seas he was doomed to disappointment, for, beyond a wireless message, relayed by a sister ship of the Empress boat, on which he was travelling, from Hong Kong, advising him that Hsui-fsi was leaving at once for that place, he received nothing else until they docked at Vancouver.

There, however, he was handed a cable in code, which, once in their rooms at the C.P.R. Hotel, they lost no time in deciphering. It ran as follows:

"Have explored every channel which seemed to offer any hope of success, but without results so far. It is practically certain that neither Wu Ling nor the Chuen-to-yan have secured possession of the vase, although, from the bits I have been able to piece together, am convinced your theory is correct, and that Carter came into possession as indicated by you. Wu Ling and agents of Chuen-to-yan been working frantically to discover whereabouts of vase, from which it seems certain they failed to discover it in Carter's luggage. Wu Ling left here ten days ago by Pacific line for San Francisco, which seems to point to fact he has hit on some clue. Advise you endeavour to keep track of him, as 'Frisco may not be final destination. Shall continue probing matter here until have exhausted every possibility, and will cable you further possibly Belmont, New York, but positively London. If any news your side cable me address you know Hong Kong. If I fail here will proceed 'Frisco next Pacific line boat two weeks hence."

Beyond practical confirmation that Blake's theory, based on what his American fellow-passenger had told him, was correct, and that both Wu Ling and the Chuen-to-yan had failed to get possession of the vase, there was not much about the message of a satisfactory nature.

True, it told them that Wu Ling had sailed for San Francisco, which as Hsui-fsi stated, seemed to point to the fact that he was following up some clue. But what that could be Blake couldn't guess, and it was out of the question for him to go down to 'Frisco to await

Wu Ling's arrival, and try to discover what he was up to. They had already been away from London for a considerable time, and there were matters there needing the most urgent attention. Therefore, Blake sent a reply to Sir Gordon advising him that they were proceeding direct overland to Montreal, from which port they would make early connection for Liverpool, and instructing him to cable to the Windsor in Montreal, instead of the Belmont in New York.

On reaching Montreal they found a brief cable from Sir Gordon, saying that he had come upon nothing further, but that his most trusted agents were working on the matter still, while he was sailing for 'Frisco.

A glance at the steamship reports in the papers showed that the Pacific line boat, by which Sir Gordon had stated he was leaving, was already at sea, so Blake did not attempt to reply. He knew that Sir Gordon's most trusted agent in Hong Kong was the ancient and wise scholar Kang Ling, who would certainly find out anything if it existed, for Blake knew him personally as an influential member of the Four Lakes Tong; and, indeed, on one occasion he had done Blake a considerable service.

Nevertheless, it was most disappointing to come up against a dead end again after the extraordinary manner in which Blake had got wind of the vase, and the knowledge that his theory was probably correct. Now, as things were, he couldn't make even a faint guess as to what had become of it, nor could he tell just what Wu Ling was up to.

But Blake felt convinced that, if he had only been able to investigate matters personally in Hong Kong, he would have struck the same clue which had apparently started Wu Ling off hot foot across the Pacific.

Once they were out of the St. Lawrence, Blake gave himself to a long and detailed review of the whole question, based on the story he had heard from the American, his slight knowledge of Carter, the messages he had received from Sir Gordon Saddler, and, lastly, his own theory.

Together he and Tinker hammered out every single point, trying to figure just what Carter could have done with the vase, since, it seemed, it had not been in his luggage.

One drawback to this sort of deduction was their ignorance as to whether the antique dealer had known the vase for the sacred Ling-tse vase, or whether it had meant to him just an exceptionally fine piece of ancient Chinese work.

In either case, he would know it must possess considerable value, and he would take care to guard it accordingly. Indeed, he had stated to the four Americans that he knew it to be an exceptionally fine piece of work. Then what could he have done with it?

It did not seem reasonable to suppose that his murderers had found it and had secreted it, with the determination to wring a good round sum out of either Wu Ling or the Chuen-to-yan. Whichever faction had been guilty of the shocking murder, Blake knew that the vase, if it had been found, would have been sent on at once to one of the powerful leaders. But the fact that agents of both had been seeking it in Hong Kong proved that Sir Gordon was right on that point.

Yet there seemed no doubt at all that all Carter's luggage had been on the car in which he had driven away from the hotel. The hotel authorities had testified to that. Hence their responsibility had ceased entirely from the moment he had paid his bill and passed over the threshold of the hotel.

This was the tenor of what Blake had stated over and over to Tinker, and he was reiterating it once more on the night before they were due to land at Liverpool, when, as they paced along the promenade deck, the lad paused and laid his hand on Blake's arm.

"I say, guv'nor, how do we know that all Mr. Carter's luggage was on the car?"

"Why, my lad, all the testimony points to that. If it hadn't been, then it would have been known by the hotel people. Or if it had been sent on to the steamer it would have been traced by now, for you may rest assured that Sir Gordon would follow up that possibility."

"I don't mean exactly that, sir. What I mean is this. More than once, when you have had articles of value in your possession, rather than keep them about you, you have sent them on to London by post. Now, is there any possibility that Mr. Carter might have done that?"

Blake swung round sharply and faced the lad.

"By heavens, Tinker, but you have made a suggestion that hadn't occurred to me, and I am sure it hadn't occurred to Sir Gordon! Good lad, good lad! Let me just think that over."

Blake started on again, his head sunk in deep thought, and so absorbed did he become in Tinker's suggestion the lad had his work cut out to keep him from colliding with other passengers who were also promenading. Round and round the deck they went, Blake's stride quickening with each round as his keen mind took apart and examined every suggestion raised by Tinker's words. At last he paused and leant over the rail.

"I don't see anything else so promising as what you have suggested, my lad," he said in a low tone. "In that may be the secret of Wu Ling's sudden departure from Hong Kong. He may have thought of that, and he may have discovered that it was so.

"In that case, if the vase were amongst other objects which Carter sent on to London by registered post, then it is little wonder that no trace of it has been found in Hong Kong. And unless he had some good reason to think the vase was no longer there, why would Wu Ling abandon the quest and leave? We know he would not. He is altogether too wily, and that Ling-tse vase means more to him just now than anything else in life.

"Now, just let us look at dates. If the parcel was sent as you suggest, it would leave by the first outward mail, which might either be by the same boat by which Carter intended to sail, or by one of the trans-Pacific steamers for England, via either America or Canada.

"Personally, I incline to think it would be sent via Canada, which would mean that it would have travelled to Vancouver by the same ship which carried us. If that were so, then, as we stayed one day in Vancouver, the parcel would be just twenty-four hours ahead of us crossing the Dominion of Canada. We had to wait a day in Montreal for this ship to sail, but I know a mail steamer cleared from Quebec to Liverpool thirty-six hours ahead of us.

"Which means the parcel in question would have been in Quebec in time to catch that mail; or in other words, if this theory should prove to be correct, then the parcel must have arrived and been delivered in London some time yesterday. In that case, we can discover the fact soon after we reach London.

"Now, as for Wu Ling. You remember, my lad, Sir Gordon said he had left Hong Kong for San Francisco ten days before the sending of the cable, which, as it was delayed twenty-four hours in transit, meant eleven days; in other words, as that telegram was dated thirteen days after we had left Hong Kong, it means we had only four days' start of Wu Ling in crossing the Pacific. Now, between Hong Kong and 'Frisco he would make up two days; while, as it is only some three thousand miles from 'Frisco to New York, as against several hundred more across Canada, he would make up not less than another day and a half. Add to that the day we were forced to wait in Montreal, and we find that Wu Ling could have reached New York just about the time we sailed from Montreal. All right.

"Now then, supposing he was able to book passage immediately by a fast liner, such as the Bretonie. If he did, then, allowing for the run we made down the St. Lawrence before we struck the gulf and the open sea, it would be quite possible for Wu Ling to reach London a full day before us, and, luck with him, he might beat us by as much as forty-eight hours.

"Which means, my lad, that if it was the discovery that Carter actually did send a parcel by registered post to London, then he has had that much start in locating it and trying to get possession of it.

"I am a little sorry I did not telegraph to Bryant Kennedy in New York, and ask him to find out if Wu Ling was sailing by one of the steamers leaving about that date. However, we can soon find out from the purser's list what ships were due to leave New York about then."

"If you are right, then Wu Ling has had lots of time to snaffle the vase, guv'nor!" remarked Tinker.

"Quite true, my lad. But he may not have been able to book passage by a steamer as quickly as he wished. In that case, it would be an even chance. At any rate, we can do one thing to ascertain if he is in London."

"What is that?"

"We shall get a wireless away to-night to our old friend Hong-Lo-Soo asking him to find out if Prince Wu Ling has arrived, and to have the advice to meet us on our arrival at Baker Street tomorrow evening. And, by the way, Tinker, don't forget to get a telegram off to Mrs. Bardell advising her that we are coming through."

"Very good, sir. Anyway, guv'nor, if Wu Ling is in London and hasn't got the vase yet, we still have a chance, and the fight isn't over, as you thought, in Canton."

"True. If the prince is in London, Tinker, whether he has the Ling-tse vase or not, the affair is not finished. I shall use every means in my power to lay him by the heels before he can get away from England with it."

Blake went off then to draft his wireless message to Hong-Lo-Soo, the wealthy Chinese merchant in Limehouse, who was a very old friend of Blake, and who, like Kang Ling, in Hong Kong, was a prominent member of the Four Lakes Tong, and who has already appeared in these pages.

And it was perfectly obvious that, through members of the Four Lakes Tong, Hong-Lo-Soo could soon discover if the prince had arrived. So when the wireless was sent, Blake and Tinker busied themselves with their packing, in order to have everything ready as soon as they should dock on the morrow. But more than once during the evening the thought crossed Blake's mind that Tinker had made a suggestion which should have occurred to him —Blake— many days before.

It pleased him no little to have seen this exhibition of the keenness with which the lad was taking his profession. They docked about eleven the next day, and as there was a boat special waiting to convey passengers and mails to London, they boarded it at once. On reaching London, they drove straight through to Baker Street, and as they drew near their own residence Tinker grinned widely and called Blake's attention to a most sumptuous Rolls-Royce which was drawn up at the kerb in front of the house, at the wheel of which was a smartly uniformed Chinese chauffeur, while beside him was an equally smart Chinese footman.

"Hong-Lo-Soo got your wireless all right, guv'nor!" he said. "One couldn't miss that outfit in a thousand, even if he does drive through to the West End only once in a blue moon! We ought to know pretty soon now whether Wu Ling is in London or not!"

Blake nodded.

"I hope he is not waiting in the car," he remarked. "And I also hope to goodness Mrs. Bardell was able to overcome her dislike of 'furriners' sufficiently to remember that he is a highly respected friend of mine and to invite him in the consulting-room!"

Tinker grinned again, for he knew only too well how difficult it was to persuade Mrs. Bardell that all yellow gentlemen were not necessarily cutthroats and fiends, such as she was prone to class them indiscriminately. As they stepped out of the taxi the footman, who recognised them, sprang down smartly and stood to attention. Blake glanced inside the Rolls-Royce and saw that it was empty.

"Please, honourable sir, my honoured master is waiting within your honourable house."

"I trust your honourable master has not been kept waiting long by our unworthy selves?" responded Blake.

"My honourable master bade me inform the honourable one that he trusted his unworthy presence would not offend you."

"My unworthy abode has been honoured," rejoined Blake; after which the footman sprang up the steps and picked up the bags which the driver had deposited there.

Blake and Tinker passed at once into the consulting-room, pausing only long enough in the hall to greet Mrs. Bardell and inquire after her well-being.

They found Hong-Lo-Soo, gorgeously clad as ever, seated in a saddlebag chair before a fire, which Mrs. Bardell had kindled, smoking one of his invariable yellow cigarettes, and perusing a monograph of Blake's which he had picked up from the table.

The merchant was evidently thoroughly at home. He laid the book down as they entered, and getting slowly to his feet, gravely saluted first Blake and then Tinker by placing his folded hands across his stomach —which is, of course, the seat of wisdom among the Chinese —and bowing low, Blake returned the bow, but refrained from the other action, while Tinker followed his master's example.

The lad was too well versed in things Celestial by now to reveal any amusement at things which would have struck him as bizarre a few years ago, and consequently sent him into paroxysms of inward mirth.

When the greetings were over, Blake courteously pressed his visitor back into his seat. Then he himself sat down at his desk, which, out of the corner of his eye, he saw was literally swamped under the avalanche of correspondence that had piled up during his absence.

"I imagine, honoured friend, that your presence here means that you received my unworthy message?" said Blake, as he opened his cigarette-case.

The merchant nodded.

"Even so, Honourable One. I at once made the inquiries which you wished. And I have succeeded in finding out that Prince Wu Ling is in London."

"Ah! Am I correct in thinking than he arrived but a few days ago?"

"Your prescience is, as ever, flawless, honoured friend. He reached London the night before last, since when he has been very actively engaged on certain business. But before I speak further of

40

him, honoured friend, permit me to speak of our mutual and esteemed friend the honourable Kang Ling, of Hong Kong."

Blake's interest quickened perceptibly. "What of the wise and much-to-be-respected one?" he asked quickly.

"Permit me to explain. Also forgive my unworthy tongue for speaking of matters which concern your person, honoured friend, but it is necessary to do so. Some days ago I received a long cable message from the wise Kang Ling in which he informed me of certain incidents which had occurred in Hong Kong and Canton. He spoke of you and of the honourable Hsui-fsi.

"I need not waste your valuable time by going into details that are more familiar to you than to me. Suffice it to say that I know what occurred at the House of Two Hundred Intelligences, in Canton. I also know of a certain murder in Hong Kong, and that the ever-to-be-reviled Wu Ling and the much-to-be-pitied Chuen-to-yan, who has been led astray, became immediately engaged in trying to trace the whereabouts of a certain object which is revered by all my countrymen.

"Like our honoured friend Kang Ling, I also believe that the policy of the wise Hsui-fsi is the best one for my poor country, and for that reason the Four Lakes Tong, to which I have the honour to belong, are working with the Three Feathers Tong to secure possession of that sacred object in order that the wise Hsui-fsi may make use of it at the right time.

"But, despite all the efforts of Hsui-fsi and Kang Ling, this object was not to be found in Hong Kong. Nor did Wu Ling or the Chuen-to-yan discover its whereabouts. It disappeared as mysteriously as it had vanished in the garden of the House of Two Hundred Intelligences, in Canton. And by the time the honourable Hsui-fsi left Hong Kong its abiding-place was still unknown.

"From his communication to me, it seems, honourable friend, that you are aware Prince Wu Ling departed from Hong Kong soon after you had sailed."

"Yes. That is how I thought it possible he had reached London."

"That had escaped my stupidity for the moment. The wise Kang Ling is of the opinion that Wu Ling made the same discovery after only a few days in Hong Kong, which he made just before sending me the cablegram. He could not cable direct to the Honourable Hsui-fsi, since our honoured friend has not yet reached San Francisco. Nor could he communicate with you, for the same reason. Therefore, he honoured my unworthy self by asking me to seek you out as soon as you arrived in order inform you of what he had discovered.''

"Forgive me, Hong-Lo-Soo, am I right in thinking that this discovery, made by the wise Kang Ling, is to the effect that the man who was murdered in Hong Kong had sent certain valuable objects, among which was the sacred one of which you have spoken, to London by registered post?"

"You are omniscient, honoured friend. My visit need not have been made. I should have known that you would discover this. It is exactly as you say."

Blake smiled as he glanced across at Tinker.

"It was not I who hit on that idea, Hong-Lo-Soo. It was my young assistant."

"In that case the young honourable one has revealed a flash of wisdom which he has received from you, honourable friend. I have observed him ere this, and I find he possesses many points of to-be-desired qualities."

Tinker flushed at the words, for it is rare indeed for a Celestial to speak any words of praise to youth. And for that reason he knew the oddly-worded compliment to be more than usually sincere, or the grave-faced merchant would never have unbent to speak it.

"That was what our honourable friend Kang Ling discovered," went on Hong-Lo-Soo. "And this is what I did, honourable friend. Knowing that, after a long absence, you would have many things to attend to, I took it upon my unworthy self to make investigations here pending your arrival. I found that the unfortunate murdered one had an honourable brother here in London, who was also a partner in the antique business, which you will surely know is conducted in a small street off Regent Street.

"It seemed wisest that I should make inquiries of him, and I set out to do so. I reached there this afternoon, and, on the pretence of making a few purchases of articles from my own country— though, I regret to say, honourable friend, many of the things he thinks are of great value are rubbish, which I would scorn to give an enemy —I secured his attention. I succeeded in gaining access to his private room, where I exhibited great interest in the ceramic ware of China, and of which I have some poor knowledge.

"It was thus that, after an interval of time, he opened a strong box, and took out a small object, about, which he asked my unworthy opinion. Honourable friend, it was then I saw that the wise Kang Ling had been right. It was the sacred object which had been posted from Hong Kong by the unfortunate man who was murdered."

"The Ling-tse vase!" breathed Blake.

"Even so, honourable friend, I said little of its qualities, sacred to my people, but I determined to endeavour to secure it at once, so that this current of crime and violence which follows it might be brought to an end. Therefore I offered what I thought the honourable antiquary might consider a good price. What do you think he did, honourable friend?"

"I cannot attempt to guess, Hong-Lo-Soo."

"He committed an unpardonable vulgarity among gentlemen of my race, honourable friend. He descended to ribaldry. He was mirthful."

"He scorned your offer?"

"That, honourable friend, is what I was led to infer by his unseemly mirth. Had it not been the sacred object, which it was greatly-to-be-treasured duty to secure. I should have departed in scorn.

"But it was necessary that I should persist. I did so, and soon discovered what had caused such a display of vulgarity. It was because another of my countrymen had been there earlier in the day, honourable friend, and had offered much more than the price I had named. It seemed most unfitting to see such a vulgar display from the brother of one who had met such a terrible end, and which we know was due to the very vase over which we were haggling. But it is my unworthy opinion, honourable friend, that the death of the brother was not unwelcome to the one who remains, since I read in his eye the soul of greed."

"Apparently not very sorry to have the whole business fall into his hands," remarked Blake, with a curl of the lip.

"That is how it seemed to me, honourable friend. And, since it was so, I immediately raised my price to a much higher figure than that which had been offered by the other."

"Did he accept it, Hong-Lo-Soo?"

"No. He informed me that if I wanted the vase sufficiently to raise my bid several thousands in one jump, it must be worth far more. He added that the other who had desired to buy it would return to-morrow, when he would probably bid much higher. I then did an unwise thing, my friend. I have never done such a thing in all my years as a merchant in China. I offered him such a price that I thought he could not refuse. It was as nothing to the value of the Ling-tse vase. No matter what heights I went to there are a hundred million of my race who would give their all to pay the price and more. I offered fifty thousand pounds. He refused."

Blake's brows went up in amazement, and well they might. Fifty thousand pounds for a tiny vase, no larger than an ordinary thimble! It had been unwise, for the veriest novice in ceramics would know that no actual value, from an antiquarian point of view, could make the vase worth anything approaching that figure; and, even if he didn't know much about the Chinese, he would guess, unless he were an utter dolt, that there was something behind it all which, if he played his cards well, would enrich him to a far greater degree than fifty thousand pounds.

Alternatively, had he known more of that intriguing race, he might have been a little uneasy at being in the possession of an article which seemed to be so much desired by powerful members of the same.

But, apparently, the brother of the murdered man was not only saturated in greed, but was a bit of a fool as well.

"Have you any idea of the identity of the other person who tried to buy it?" asked Blake, after a brief pause.

"I should have had none were it not for the receipt of your wireless message, honourable friend. I am now certain that it was Wu Ling."

"I suspected so. And he is to return to-morrow?"

"So I have been informed."

"Then we must see this man Carter this evening, Hong-Lo-Soo. Where one of your honourable race might fail to secure the vase, I may be able to impress him with the fact that it is essential, for other reasons besides his own safety, that he disposes of the vase to me this night at whatever figure in reason he wishes to name. If he refuses, then I shall be forced to pull certain strings which, I fancy, will make him only too anxious to do as I request."

"That, honourable friend, is exactly what was in my own unworthy mind. For that reason I brought my poor person into your honourable house to wait. My unworthy vehicle (his sumptuous

Rolls-Royce) is waiting, and I shall be honoured if you and the young honourable one will enter it."

"We shall do so without delay, Hong-Lo-Soo. Everything must wait on this matter of the Ling-tse vase."

They rose then, and, without waiting for the usual amenities of refreshment, they passed out to the street and entered the waiting car. Hong-Lo-Soo gave the address through an ivory-mouthed speaking-tube, and a moment later the car glided away from the kerb.

There was scarcely a word spoken on the way, each being occupied with his own thoughts.

Just how Hong-Lo-Soo's mind might be functioning it would be difficult to say, but one thing was certain, by his own devious mental process he was arriving at exactly the same conclusion as Blake and Tinker, which was that, by hook or by crook, the Ling-tse vase must be theirs that night. Each one of the three knew to what extent the fanatical Wu Ling would accept a refusal on the part of a person of Carter's calibre.

They found the little street into which they turned, after leaving Regent Street, almost deserted, and it occurred to Blake that they might find the antique shop closed. As if he had read Blake's thoughts; the Celestial turned and said: "When the idea came to me in your honourable abode before your arrival, honourable friend, I took the liberty of using your telephone. I informed the antiquary that I was returning this evening to make a new offer, and his greed impelled him to wait. We shall find him in the place."

A few seconds later the car drew up in front of the shop.

Blake had made an occasional purchase from the brother who had been murdered, but he had not visited the shop very often, and, to his recollection, had never encountered the brother whom they were now about to see. After a little collision of courtesies, Hong-Lo-Soo consented to enter the place first.

The door was closed, but not locked. Inside a single light was burning, but through a half-open door at the rear they could see a brighter light. It was towards this Hong-Lo-Soo walked.

As he reached it he raised his hand and knocked. There was no reply; so, after a few moments, he pushed gently against the panels. The door swung inwards, and Hong-Lo-Soo crossed the threshold, followed closely by Blake and Tinker. But just over the threshold all three paused at the ghastly sight which met their gaze.

Lying huddled up on the floor, with a knife driven to the hilt in his throat, amid a great pool of spreading crimson, was the body of a man. To the experienced eyes of that trio it was plain that he had not been dead long, and they knew that, even as they had talked at Baker Street, someone had entered the shop and had driven that blade of death into the throat of the antiquarian, for that it was he Blake knew from the likeness to the other.

The drawers in the desk had been dragged open, and the contents lay scattered about the place. And over to the right was a strong box, with the door swinging open. It was that sight which told them the motive of this ghastly crime which had been perpetrated so recently.

It was that sight which told them that once more the Ling-tse vase was gone!

Hong-Lo-Soo did not glance towards the huddled heap on the floor as he passed it and picked up the desk telephone. Blake and Tinker approached the safe, and from their examination it was soon plain that it had not been forced open by any form of explosive. Some master-hand had discovered the secret of the combination. (*Chapter 6.*)

Sexton Blake went up the stairs two at a time, regardless of the fight that was raging beneath. One of the Celestials had detached himself from the throng and was racing for cover on the floor above. After winging one of the defenders, Tinker dashed up after his master. (*Chapter* 6.)

HONG-LO-SOO was the first to break the spell which had fallen on them at the scene.

"Honoured friend," he said, in the same expressionless tones which he employed for ordinary conversation, "this is undoubtedly a matter for your great honourable police. But do you agree with my unworthy opinion that it is the work of the accursed one, Wu Ling, of the equally-to-be-detested Tong of the Brotherhood of the Yellow Beetle?"

"That is my opinion, Hong-Lo-Soo," assented Blake gravely.

"In that case, will you permit me to act first? As you see, honourable friend, the deed has been committed but recently. The slayer cannot have had time to reach safety. There is a chance that we may be able to cut him off if I send word through at once, and have every available man of the Four Lakes Tong and the Three Feather Tong throw out the net. They can act much more swiftly than your honourable police. Have I your honourable consent?"

"Most assuredly, my friend. In the meantime, my assistant and I shall make an examination of the safe."

Hong-Le-Soo did not glance towards the huddled heap on the floor as he passed it and picked up the desk telephone. While he was so engaged, Blake and Tinker approached the safe and began to make an examination. It was soon plain to them that it had not been forced by any form of explosive, but that a master-hand had soon discovered the secret of the combination.

Inside, there were a few, obviously valuable, antique objects; but, search as they would, they could find no sign of the Ling-tse vase, and, because he knew instinctively that it was gone, Blake soon desisted.

As they rose they could hear Hong-Lo-Soo still talking through the telephone.

He was speaking in Chinese, and at such a rate that it was difficult for Blake to follow him, but he gathered that the influential merchant was issuing instructions which would be flashed round the whole Chinatown of London in far less time than it would have taken Blake to get to Scotland Yard to get the great police-net into action. He knew Hong-Lo-Soo had only stated a fact when he said that, if they hoped at all to cut off the murderer before he could take cover,

48

the only way was to set his own race after him.

When Hong-Lo-Soo had finished, Blake took up the receiver and called Scotland Yard. He got through to Inspector Thomas, with whom he had worked on so many cases, and in a few words explained to that efficient official what they had discovered in the antique shop. In response to the inspector's question, as to whether he would find Blake at the shop when he came, Blake answered that he proposed following up a clue in the East End, and arranged that Scotland Yard should have a flying cordon in readiness to proceed at a moment's notice to whatever point Blake should designate so soon as he himself should know.

Then they left the shop; but, before driving off, Blake walked along to Regent Street, where he informed the constable on the beat what they had found, and explained that Inspector Thomas would be on the scene in a few minutes. The constable went back to the shop to take charge, and then, at a word from Kong-Lo-Soo, the car started for the East End.

Twice they were held up for violating the speed limit; but as soon as Blake bad been identified, and had given a satisfactory assurance as to the need, they were permitted to proceed. It was plain that Hong-Lo-Soo had a definite objective in mind, for he paid no attention to the course they were following until they were well into Limehouse.

There, as they entered a small, silent square, the car drew up, and it had scarcely come to rest when out of the shadows a figure glided. The man approached the car and bowed low as the footman opened the door. He spoke a few words to Hong-Lo-Soo, who merely grunted, after which the footman closed the door and sprang back to his place.

The car moved on again then; but Hong-Lo-Soo did not communicate to Blake and Tinker what message he had received from his agent, nor whither they were bound. But it was plain that he had some definite objective in view, for the car turned frequently as it got deeper into the quarter, and, as they peered out of the windows into the murky night, the two detectives recognised only too well the unsavoury nature of their surroundings.

In itself, the night was not unlike that one on which Blake and Hsui-fsi had emerged from the Temple of Eternal Light. Such conditions seemed in some fateful way to surround all their doings in connection with the Ling-tse vase.

Even though their chase had led them half-way across the globe, from the Thieves' Market of Canton to the East End of London, there was still the breath of the Yellow Empire over all. There was the hint of an uneasy spirit which, it seemed, must dwell in that mysterious vessel that had been of unknown antiquity even far, far back in the famous Wei dynasty, when the culture of China had reached its zenith, and when the Roman was building his amphitheatres in conquered Gaul and savage Britain.

And yet here, in the very heart of the stupendous Empire which had been built up by the extraordinary race evolved in the little western island, was that same vase still luring men on to destruction in the lust for power and dominion which was kindled aeons ago in the breasts of our simian ancestors.

It was when they turned into a narrow and gloomy cul-de-sac that the car again stopped, and once more a shadowy figure glided towards them. This time the parleying continued some time longer, and at the end of it Hong-Lo-Soo turned to Blake.

"It is well that I had your permission to act at once, honourable friend," he said in a low tone. "My men have succeeded in cutting off the one we seek. He has been forced into cover close at hand, and my cordon extends about the whole quarter. If you are ready, it is for us to take him, if you will."

Blake smiled to himself in the shadow.

If he hadn't known Hong-Lo-Soo so well, he might have been tempted to think that the Chinese merchant was a little boastful, for, although he spoke of having thrown a cordon completely round the quarter, there wasn't a single person to be seen, with the exception of the one who had approached the car. But he knew Hong-Lo-Soo, and he knew that if the latter stated their man was surrounded, then it was a fact.

And, since he was extraordinarily keen to lay the murderer by the heels before he could reach Wu Ling, he wasted no time in questions. He simply murmured a quick assent, and Hong-Lo-Soo stepped out of the car, followed by Blake and Tinker.

A few more words between the merchant and the agent, then Hong-Lo-Soo turned and gave a few curt instructions to the chauffeur. They stood waiting while the car turned and drove off. Then they moved on down the cul-de-sac, Hong-Lo-Soo informing Blake as they went that the last house but one on the left was their objective.

And then, in a most startling manner, the whole narrow cul-de-sac began, literally, to swarm with stealthy yellow forms.

They poured in, in a shadowy stream, from the mouth of the lane; they appeared suddenly from every dark corner where they had been blotted from sight by the heavy black of the background. They emerged from those silent, dark-shuttered houses with scarcely a sound. There must have been not less than two hundred of them, and Blake knew, too, that there would be an equal number behind the house where their man had taken refuge. But would they find Wu Ling there? Not even Hong-Lo-Soo could tell him yet.

After a few whispered words Blake advised attacking suddenly. The Chinaman agreed to this, and uttered a single word, which was quickly taken up and carried along among the ranks.

A few fugitive shafts of light now showed on shining blades as weapons were drawn, and, following that, Blake and Tinker, with automatics ready, and Hong-Lo-Soo with nothing in his hand but a half-open fan, led the way to the black oblong that marked the porch.

It was evident that no attempt was to be made to gain admittance to the place through strategy.

What sort of force might be hidden inside no one could tell, nor, while both Blake and Hong-Lo-Soo were equally agreed that the murder of the second Carter had undoubtedly been the work of Wu Ling, they did not for a moment believe that the prince had actually committed the deed.

Wu Ling would be far too cautious to compromise himself to that extent, when it was so easy for him to command the execution of the murder by any one of the numerous members of the Brotherhood of the Yellow Beetle resident in the East End. This house which faced them might be where the prince had lain in wait for the tool he had employed to come to him and give him the vase.

Or, as Hong-Lo-Soo had opined, the fellow had been cut off by his men before he could reach Wu Ling. In that case, even if they succeeded in bagging the actual murderer —even if they were so fortunate as to gain possession of the Ling-tse vase —there was still Wu Ling to consider, and with Blake the capture of the prince ranked only very little below the recovery of the vase. Therefore he was keenly impatient to discover just what those black walls before them concealed.

It wasn't to be long before his curiosity was satisfied.

At a sign from Hong-Lo-Soo about a score of Celestials crowded into the porch, and the next instant that cul-de-sac, that had been so sinister and silent, was filled with a sudden pandemonium of yells as the assault began.

It was enough for the Chinese merchant's men to know that, for once in their lives, they were acting on the side of governing authority, and that the tall, grim-faced man who accompanied their chief was acting on behalf of the law they would just as readily have scouted, for them to seize the chance to come to grips with the opposing faction.

As if it had been made of cardboard, the door crashed in, and, on the heels of the human battering-ram, Hong-Lo-Soo, Blake, and Tinker were swept into the lower hall of the house.

Outside the shuttered windows had revealed no signs of life, but now, as they poured over the threshold, Blake could see that the lower hall was lighted by a single hanging lamp, while straight ahead of them was a door which was jerked open as they plunged in.

A single glimpse served to show that it was literally packed with Celestials, who now advanced to meet the invaders with knives drawn.

Which of them might be the man they more particularly wanted to reach Blake did not know until, just as the besieged rushed upon them, a Celestial, who had clung close to the side of Hong-Lo-Soo, gave a cry, and pointed to one of the figures which had detached itself from the others, and, flying over the balustrade, was racing up the stairs to the floor above. Hong-Lo-Soo pointed the man out to Blake, and, as the two bodies crashed together, Blake shouted to Tinker and made for the stairs.

He went up them two at a time, regardless of the melee that was now raging beneath. Tinker managed to slip through after winging one of the defending party, and raced after Blake. Guarded by his own personal bodyguard, and with his incongruous fan waving slowly back and forth, utterly oblivious of the knives that were flashing about him, Hong-Lo-Soo, as deliberately as if he were making a ceremonial visit, began also to mount.

By now Blake had reached the top, and was just in time to kick open a door which the fugitive attempted to slam in his face. Tinker reached him just then, and together the two of them sent the door crashing inwards. Inside they saw their man at bay in one corner. He had dragged a table in front of him, and was standing with knife ready to hurl.

Indeed, even as they entered, Blake jerked his head aside just in time to avoid the flashing blade which skimmed past his neck and stuck quivering in the wall. Tinker gave a grunt of anger, and took a pot shot at the Celestial, who gave a yell as the bullet thudded into his arm, smashing the bone to splinters.

It was just then that Hong-Lo-Soo reached the open door, and it was he who, for once, quickened his mode of expression sufficiently to cry quickly to Blake:

"The vase, honourable friend! Watch him. He means mischief!"

It was well that Hong-Lo-Soo spoke when he did, for, despite the smashed arm, which had dropped to his side, the cornered Chinaman had managed to get his free hand inside his jacket, and, even as Hong-Lo-Soo finished speaking, his hand came out, holding the precious Ling-tse vase between finger and thumb. Then even the two Europeans in that strange drama gave a gasp of horror as the Celestial lifted his arm and deliberately hurled the sacred vase away from him, directly at the floor in front of where they stood.

It seemed as if at long last the Ling-tse vase had ended its course, that after thousands of years its trail of blood and intrigue was ended. It seemed that nothing could intervene in that brief span of time between the moment it left the hand of the destroyer to the instant when it would be shattered to pieces on the floor.

Nor would it have been possible if one of those two Europeans had not been no mean exponent of the classic game of cricket, for, scarcely had the vase left the fingers of the murderer, than Tinker launched himself forward, his hand shooting out like a flash, and his fingers closing round the vase the barest fraction of a second before it struck.

Over and over he rolled with the force of his dive, until he crashed against the table behind which the murderer had taken cover. With a shrill squeal of rage the Celestial jerked out a second knife, and bent forward to hurl it down upon the momentarily helpless lad. But before he could do so there came a second flash, something whirred between Blake and Hong-Lo-Soo, and the Celestial staggered back as the point of the blade ripped deep into his throat.

He went down with a crash, the front of his jacket crimsoning in a wide stain as he fell.

Tinker scrambled to his feet, and gingerly opened his hand to see if the vase was really uninjured. He grinned as he held it up.

"How's that, umpire?"

Blake strode across and took the vase, which he examined swiftly.

"But for you it would have been but a shattered ruin, my lad," he said jerkily.

Hong Lo-Soo was beside them fanning himself as imperturbably as ever, but in his wise old eyes there was a new look of respect as he laid his hand on Tinker's shoulder.

"Young honourable one," he said slowly and impressively, "you know not what you have done this night. But my honourable country, that which is best in it, will count itself blood-brother to you from now. It is not here that I would speak, but anon, when I have communicated what you have done, you shall find that the gratitude of millions may be expressed as strongly as the enmity of those same millions. Elder that I am, I salute you."

Which was about the most emphatic way a Celestial could express his emotion, which, though it was not exhibited outwardly, was, nevertheless, stirring Hong-Lo-Soo to his very depths. He had actually witnessed what seemed inevitable destruction of what was almost the most sacred and powerful symbol of all China. He had seen it snatched from destruction as if by a miracle.

And, a few months later, Tinker did indeed receive a most emphatic recognition of gratitude. So emphatic, so colossal was it that it needed all Hong-Lo-Soo's powers of persuasion, based, on Blake's own knowledge of the Chinese, to gain his consent that Tinker should accept it.

But even more than that was an ancient-looking parchment, covered with most intriguing characters, which made Tinker a "seventh elder" of the two most powerful tongs in China. When one considers that this admittance gave him the undeniable right to summon to his service several millions of Celestials who would do his bidding, no matter what it might be, some little idea can be gained as to just how valuable that might prove to him in the future.

Blake insisted that Hong-Lo-Soo should take charge of the vase. Then, with the merchant still waving his fan before him, they proceeded to see how things had progressed on the floor below. It stood to reason that, with overwhelming numbers in their favour, the melee could not last long. But as they descended the stairs it was evident that the invaders had not yielded without a most determined defence.

The dead and wounded were lying about in every direction, while a double line of Hong-Lo-Soo's men were keeping a way clear to the door. There would be a good deal of cleaning up to do before the signs of the fracas would be cleared away, and there would be some searching police investigations before it was over.

But that was no affair of Blake's.

He had gone after a murderer, and the man had paid the penalty of his deed. He had gone after the Ling-tse vase, and, thanks to Tinker's snap-catch, they had secured it. Now, the sooner they were out of the place the better. And it was with a decided sigh of relief that he sank back in the Rolls-Royce and felt it move off swiftly.

At Hong-Lo-Soo's place of business they waited for some time for reports of Wu Ling's whereabouts. But nothing came through, despite the fact that the merchant's agents were scouring the East End in every direction. It became imperative for Blake and Tinker to go on and make their statement to Scotland Yard regarding the murder of the antique dealer, so, after taking leave of Hong-Lo-Soo, and arranging that he should send word to Baker Street immediately Wu Ling was located, they drove off. But neither the next day nor the next did that message come.

•   •   •   •   •

On the third day, however, a brief note came from Hong-Lo-Soo, couched in guarded terms, but sufficient to tell Blake that Wu Ling had, in some way, managed to slip through the net, and had succeeded in getting away from England. Blake tossed the message to Tinker with a shrug, and returned to the work which was occupying him at the moment.

Tinker frowned as he read, but he knew that it was useless to ask Blake if he would follow. He knew that, for the time being at least, they would be unable to leave England, so, with a muttered imprecation, he bent over the "Index" on which he had been engaged.

At that same instant both Blake and Tinker might have been mildly interested to observe the doings of several others who had been mixed up in that long drawn-out drama of the Ling-tse vase, for, the day following its recovery, the news had been cabled to those interested, and it was a safe bet that the Chuen-to-yan had also heard the startling intelligence.

As a matter of fact, in the privacy of his private office, the merchant, Hong-Lo-Soo, was gravely engaged in inditing a flowery epistle to the ever-to-be-respected Hsui-fsi, detailing to him the miraculous manner in which the vase had been saved.

．　．　．　．　．

Night in San Francisco and in the House of the Silver Moon, the ancient Hsui-fsi was seated cross-legged upon his silken divan, an open cable message before him. At his elbow stood a Chinese "boy," preparing the "pipe," the first with which Hsui-fsi was about to begin one of those bouts which had shrivelled him to the likeness of a yellow mummy.

But not yet had his mind drifted into the fairy realms of drugged ecstasy, and, as he laid the cablegram aside, his thoughts went to that other ancient who was sitting upon the throne of the Chuen-to-yan, of the Temple of Eternal Light, in Canton. And, in the contemplation of that, his wrinkled features twisted up in alarming manner, while his frail form shook with silent mirth.

．　．　．　．　．

Morning in Hong Kong.

Before his small, squat lacquered table was seated the learned Kang Ling. On the table was a pot of fragrant Suchow tea, and beside it a dish of Santok almonds. He had just finished his devotions, and now he was engaged in pondering over one of the Five Classics.

It was a most intricate bit of philosophy which could only be understood by one who was approaching the ascetic state known as Bodivasta; but the learned old gentleman seemed to find tremendous interest in it, and had one been able to follow him, one might have noticed that his eyes rested longest on those few occasions when mention was made of the sacred Ling-tse vase.

．　．　．　．　．

Morning also in Canton.

Seated on his throne, in the underground apartment of the Temple of Eternal Light, was the Chuen-to-yan. From somewhere above him came the distant sound of the temple gongs, broken from time to time by the harsh blare of a trumpet. He was as motionless as the statue of the Buddha which towered above him.

And if one could have gazed upon him at that moment one might have believed that he had indeed been seated thus for the hundred and fifty years which rumour gave it he had ruled as the Chuen-to-yan.

What tortuous thoughts might be passing behind that wide dome no living being could guess. But if mind could have read there would have been found imprinted on that extraordinary brain the form of the Ling-tse vase.

And where was Wu Ling?

Across the Bay of Biscay a small tramp steamer was lumbering along like a drunken porpoise. Forward, a solitary figure stood alone, gazing broodingly at the grey water which churned and drove against the blunt bows. Behind him lay a path of death and intrigue. Before him lay a misty curtain, beyond which he could not see.

But, so surely as night must go and day must conquer, so surely must Wu Ling go on in the way he had chosen, utterly oblivious of the wreckage which would mark his passage. Go on, yes, until one day he should at last be overwhelmed by the man who sat at that moment in the consulting-room at Baker Street, as cool and calculating and as implacable in the service of justice as a machine — but a machine with a heart and brain.

THE END.
[22000 WORDS]

It seemed as if, at long last, the Ling-tse vase had ended its course, and that, after thousands of years, its trail of blood and intrigue had ended. For the Celestial had lifted his arm suddenly and hurled it at the floor. It seemed as if nothing could intervene to save it. But Tinker flung himself forward, shot out his arm, and felt his fingers close round it the barest fraction of a second before it struck. (*Chapter 6.*)

www.ingramcontent.com/pod-product-compliance
Lightning Source LLC
Chambersburg PA
CBHW020341130626
46549CB00003B/1238